Tigger
three books in one

Tigger Has Breakfast

Based on the stories of A. A. Milne

Winnie-the-Pooh woke up suddenly in the middle of the night and listened. He got out of bed, lit his candle, and went to see if anybody was trying to get into his honey-cupboard. They weren't so he got back into bed. Then he heard the noise again.

"Is that you, Piglet?" he said.

But it wasn't.

The noise went on.

"*Worraworraworraworraworra,*" it said.

"There are lots of noises in the Forest, but this is different," thought Pooh. "It isn't a growl, and it isn't a purr, but it's a noise of some kind, made by a strange animal! I shall get up and ask him not to do it."

He got out of bed and opened his front door.

"Hallo!" said Pooh.

"Hallo!" said Whatever-it-was.

"Who is it?" Pooh asked.

"Me," said the strange voice.

In the candle-light, Whatever-it-was and Pooh looked at each other.

"I'm Pooh," said Pooh.

"I'm Tigger," said Tigger.

Pooh had never seen an animal like this before. "Does Christopher Robin know about you?"

"Of course he does," said Tigger.

"Well," said Pooh, "it's the middle of the night which is a good time for going to sleep. Tomorrow morning we'll have some honey for breakfast. Do Tiggers like honey?"

"They like everything," said Tigger cheerfully.

"Then if they like going to sleep on the floor, I'll go back to bed," said Pooh, "and we'll do things in the morning. Good night."

And he got back into bed and went fast asleep.

In the morning, the first thing Pooh saw was Tigger, sitting in front of the mirror, looking at himself.

"I've found somebody just like me. I thought I was the only one of them," said Tigger.

Pooh began to explain what a mirror was, but just as he was getting to the interesting part, Tigger said:

"Excuse me a moment, but there's something climbing up your table," and with one loud "*Worraworraworraworraworra*" he leapt up and pulled the tablecloth to the ground. After a terrible struggle, he said: "Have I won?"

"That's my tablecloth," said Pooh, as he began to unwind Tigger.

"I wondered what it was," said Tigger.

"It goes on the table and you put things on it."

"Then why did it try to bite me when I wasn't looking?"

"It didn't," said Pooh.

Pooh put the cloth back on the table, placed a honey-pot on the cloth, and they sat down to breakfast.

Tigger took a large mouthful of honey. He looked up at the ceiling with his head on one side, and made exploring noises with his tongue...and then he said:

"Tiggers don't like honey."

"Oh!" said Pooh, trying to sound sad. Pooh felt rather pleased about this, and said that when he had finished his own breakfast, he would take Tigger round to Piglet's house, and Tigger could try some haycorns.

"Thank you, Pooh, because haycorns are really what Tiggers like best."

Off they set and Pooh explained as they went that Piglet was a Very Small Animal who didn't like bouncing, and asked Tigger not to be too Bouncy at first.

Tigger said that Tiggers were only bouncy before breakfast, and that as soon as they had had a few haycorns they became Quiet and Refined.

They knocked on the door of Piglet's house.

"Hallo, Piglet. This is Tigger."

"Oh, is it?" said Piglet. "I thought Tiggers were smaller than that."

"Not the big ones," said Tigger.

"They like haycorns," said Pooh, "so that's what we've come for, because poor Tigger hasn't had any breakfast yet."

"Help yourself," said Piglet.

After a long munching noise Tigger said:

"Ee-ers o i a-ors."

Then he said: "Skoos ee," and went outside.

When he came back in he said: "Tiggers don't like haycorns."

"But you said they liked everything except honey," said Pooh.

"Everything except honey *and* haycorns," explained Tigger.

Piglet, who was rather glad that Tiggers didn't like haycorns, said, "What about thistles?"

"Thistles," said Tigger, "are what Tiggers like best."

So the three of them set off to find Eeyore.

"Hallo, Eeyore!" said Pooh. "This is Tigger."

"What is?" said Eeyore.

"This," explained Pooh and Piglet together. Tigger smiled.

"He's just come," explained Piglet.

Eeyore thought for a long time and then said: "When is he going?"

Pooh explained that Tigger was a great friend of Christopher Robin's, who had come to stay in the Forest; and Piglet explained to Tigger that he mustn't mind what Eeyore said because he was *always* gloomy; and Tigger explained to anybody who was listening that he hadn't had any breakfast yet.

"I knew there was something," said Pooh. "That was why we came to see you, Eeyore."

"Then come this way, Tigger," said Eeyore.

Eeyore led the way to a patch of thistles, and waved a hoof at it.

"A little patch I was keeping for my birthday," he said, "but what *are* birthdays? Help yourself, Tigger."

Tigger thanked him and looked at Pooh.

"Are these really thistles?" he whispered.

"Yes," said Pooh.

"What Tiggers like best?"

"That's right," said Pooh.

So Tigger took a large mouthful, and he gave a large crunch.

"*Ow!*" said Tigger.

He sat down and put his paw in his mouth.

"What's the matter?" asked Pooh.

"*Hot!*" mumbled Tigger.

He stopped shaking his head to get the prickles out, and explained that Tiggers didn't like thistles.

"But you *said* that Tiggers liked everything except honey and haycorns," said Pooh.

"*And* thistles," said Tigger, who was now running round in circles with his tongue hanging out.

Pooh looked at him sadly.

"What are we going to do?" he asked Piglet.

Piglet said at once that they must go and see Christopher Robin.

"You'll find him with Kanga," said Eeyore. He came close to Pooh, and said in a loud whisper:

"*Could* you ask your friend to do his exercises somewhere else? I shall be having lunch directly, and don't want it bounced on just before I begin. A trifling matter but we all have our little ways."

Pooh called to Tigger.

"Come along and we'll go and see Kanga. She's sure to have lots of breakfast for you."

Tigger rushed off, excitedly.

As Pooh and Piglet walked after him, Pooh thought of a poem:

What shall we do about
poor little Tigger?
If he never eats nothing
he'll never get bigger.
He doesn't like honey and
haycorns and thistles
Because of the taste and
because of the bristles.
And all the good things
which an animal likes
Have the wrong sort of swallow
or too many spikes.

"He's quite big enough anyhow," said Piglet.

Pooh thought about this, and then he murmured to himself:

But whatever his weight in pounds,
shillings, and ounces,
He always seems bigger because
of his bounces.

"And that's the poem," said Pooh. "Do you like it?"

"All except the shillings," said Piglet. "They oughtn't to be there."

"They wanted to come in after the pounds," explained Pooh, "so I let them. It is the best way to write poetry."

At last they came to Kanga's house, and there was Christopher Robin.

"Oh, there you are, Tigger!" said Christopher Robin. "I knew you'd be somewhere."

"I've been finding things in the Forest," said Tigger importantly. "I've found a pooh and a piglet and an eeyore, but I can't find any breakfast."

Pooh and Piglet explained what had happened.

"Don't *you* know what Tiggers like?" asked Pooh.

"I expect if I thought very hard I should," said Christopher Robin, "but I *thought* Tigger knew."

So they went into Kanga's house. They told Kanga what they wanted, and Kanga said very kindly, "Well, look in my cupboard, Tigger dear, and see what you'd like."

She knew at once that, however big Tigger seemed to be, he wanted as much kindness as Roo.

"Shall I look, too?" said Pooh, who was beginning to feel a little eleven o'clockish. And he found a small tin of condensed milk (that he thought Tiggers wouldn't like) and took it into a corner by itself.

But the more Tigger put his nose into this and his paw into that, the more things he found which Tiggers didn't like.

And when he had found everything in the cupboard, and couldn't eat any of it, he said to Kanga, "What happens now?"

But Kanga and Christopher Robin and Piglet were all watching Roo have his Extract of Malt. And Kanga was saying, "Now, Roo dear, you promised."

"What is it?" whispered Tigger to Piglet.

"His Strengthening Medicine," said Piglet. "He hates it."

So Tigger came closer, and he leant over the back of Roo's chair.

Then suddenly he put out his tongue, and took one large galollop, which made Kanga jump with surprise. "Oh!" she said, and then clutched at the spoon just as it was disappearing, and pulled it safely back out of Tigger's mouth. But the Extract of Malt had gone.

"He's taken my medicine, he's taken my medicine!" sang Roo happily.

Then Tigger looked up at the ceiling, and closed his eyes, and his tongue went round his chops, in case he had left any outside, and a peaceful smile came over his face as he said, "So *that's* what Tiggers like!"

Which explains why he always lived at Kanga's house afterwards, and had Extract of Malt for breakfast, dinner, and tea. And sometimes, when Kanga thought he wanted strengthening, he had a spoonful or two of Roo's breakfast after meals as medicine.

"But *I* think," said Piglet to Pooh, "that he's been strengthened quite enough."

Tiggers Don't Climb Trees

One day, when Pooh was sitting on a stone in the middle of the stream, thinking, he thought he would go and see Eeyore. He walked along, singing a little song to himself, when he thought he would go and see Owl instead as he hadn't seen him since the day before yesterday. But then he remembered Kanga, Roo and Tigger. And, of course, there was Rabbit. "I like talking to Rabbit," thought Pooh. Before he knew it, Pooh was back at his own front door again. And it was eleven o'clock. Which was Time-for-a-little-something....

Half an hour later he was doing what he had always really meant to do, he was stumping off to Piglet's house.

Piglet was busy digging a small hole in the ground outside his house.

"Hallo, Piglet," said Pooh. "What are you doing?"

"I'm planting a haycorn, Pooh, so that it can grow up into an oak-tree, and have lots of haycorns just outside the front door instead of having to walk miles and miles, do you see, Pooh?"

"Supposing it doesn't?" said Pooh.

"It will, because Christopher Robin says it will, so that's why I'm planting it."

And he put the acorn in the hole he had made, and covered it up with earth, and jumped on it.

When Piglet had finished jumping, he wiped his paws on his front, and said, "What shall we do now?" and Pooh said, "Let's go and see Kanga and Roo and Tigger." So they set off for Kanga's house.

Now, Kanga had felt rather motherly that morning, and wanted to count things – like Roo's vests, and how many pieces of soap there were left; so she sent them out with a packet of watercress sandwiches for Roo and a packet of extract-of-malt sandwiches for Tigger, to have a nice long morning in the Forest not getting into mischief. And off they had gone.

And as they went, Tigger told Roo all about the things that Tiggers could do.

"Can they fly?" asked Roo.

"Yes," said Tigger, "they're very good flyers, Tiggers are. Strornry good flyers."

"Oo!" said Roo. "Can they fly as well as Owl?"

"Yes," said Tigger. "Only they don't want to."

Roo couldn't understand this, because he thought it would be lovely to be able to fly, but Tigger said it was difficult to explain to anybody who wasn't a Tigger himself.

"Can they jump as far as Kangas?" asked Roo.

"Yes," said Tigger. "When they want to."

In a little while they came to the Six Pine Trees.

"I can swim," said Roo. "Can Tiggers swim?"

"Of course they can. Tiggers can do everything."

"Can they climb trees better than Pooh?" asked Roo, stopping under the tallest Pine Tree, and looking up at it.

"Climbing trees is what they do best," said Tigger. "Much better than Poohs."

"Could they climb this one?"

"I'll show you," said Tigger bravely, "and you can sit on my back and watch me."

"Oo, Tigger!" squeaked Roo excitedly.

So he sat on Tigger's back and up they went.

For the first ten feet Tigger said happily to himself, "Up we go!"

For the next ten feet he said:

"I always *said* Tiggers could climb trees."

And for the next ten feet he said:

"Not that it's easy, mind you."

And for the next ten feet he said:

"Of course, there's the coming down too. Backwards."

And then he said:

"Which will be difficult ..."

"Unless one fell ..."

"When it would be ..."

"EASY."

And at the word "easy", the branch he was standing on broke and he just managed to clutch at the one above him as he felt himself going....

Slowly he scrambled upwards ... until at last he was sitting on it, breathing quickly, and wishing that he had gone in for swimming instead.

Roo climbed off, and sat down next to him.

"Tigger," he said excitedly, "are we at the top?"

"No," said Tigger.

"Are we going to the top?"

"*No*," said Tigger.

"Oh!" said Roo rather sadly. Then he went on hopefully: "That was a lovely bit when you pretended we were going to fall-bump-to-the-bottom, and we didn't. Will you do that bit again?"

"NO," said Tigger.

Roo was silent for a little while, and then he said, "Shall we eat our sandwiches, Tigger?" And Tigger said, "Yes, where are they?" And Roo said, "At the bottom of the tree." And Tigger said, "I don't think we'd better eat them just yet." So they didn't.

By-and-by Pooh and Piglet came walking along.

"Look, Pooh!" said Piglet suddenly. "There's something in one of the Pine Trees."

"So there is!" said Pooh, looking up wonderingly. "There's an Animal."

Piglet took Pooh's arm, in case Pooh was frightened.

"Is it One of the Fiercer Animals?" he said, looking the other way.

Pooh nodded.

"It's a Jagular," he said.

"What do Jagulars do?" asked Piglet, hoping that they wouldn't.

"They hide in the branches of trees, and drop on you as you go underneath," said Pooh. "Christopher Robin told me."

Suddenly the Jagular called out to them.

"Help! Help!" it called.

"That's what Jagulars always do," said Pooh knowledgeably.

Something very excited next to the Jagular heard him and squeaked:

"Pooh and Piglet! Pooh and Piglet!"

"Pooh!" Piglet cried. "I believe it's Tigger and Roo!"

"So it is," said Pooh. "I thought it was a Jagular and another Jagular."

"What are you doing?" called Piglet.

"We can't get down, we can't get down!" cried Roo.

"How did you get there, Roo?" asked Piglet.

"On Tigger's back! And Tiggers can't climb downwards, because their tails get in the way, and Tigger forgot about that when we started, and he's only just remembered. So we've got to stay here for ever and ever – unless we go higher. What did you say, Tigger? Oh, Tigger says if we go higher we shan't be able to see Piglet's house so well, so we're going to stop here."

"Piglet," said Pooh solemnly, "I think they're stuck." And he began to eat Tigger's sandwiches.

"Couldn't you climb up to them?"
asked Piglet.

"I might, Piglet, and I might
bring Roo down on my back, but
I couldn't bring Tigger down.
We must think of something else."
In a thoughtful way he began to
eat Roo's sandwiches, as well.

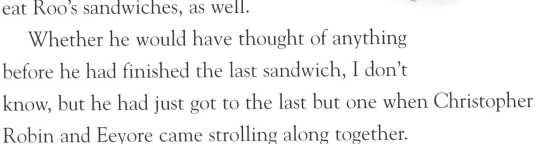

Whether he would have thought of anything
before he had finished the last sandwich, I don't
know, but he had just got to the last but one when Christopher
Robin and Eeyore came strolling along together.

"There's Pooh!" said Christopher Robin. "Hallo, Pooh!"

"It's Christopher Robin!" said Piglet. "*He'll* know what to do."

They hurried up to him.

"Oh, Christopher Robin," began Pooh.

"And Eeyore," said Eeyore.

"Tigger and Roo are up the Six Pine Trees, and they can't get down, and –"

"And I was just saying," put in Piglet, "that if only Christopher Robin –"

"*And* Eeyore –"

"If only you were here, then we could think of something to do."

Christopher Robin looked up at Tigger and Roo, and tried to think of something.

"*I* thought," said Piglet earnestly, "that if Eeyore stood at the bottom of the tree, and if Pooh stood on Eeyore's back, and if I stood on Pooh's shoulders –"

"And if Eeyore's back snapped suddenly, then we could all laugh," said Eeyore.

"Would it break your back, Eeyore?" asked Pooh, surprised.

"That's what would be so interesting – not being quite sure till afterwards."

Pooh said "Oh!" and they all began to think again.

"I've got an idea!" cried Christopher Robin suddenly. "I'll take off my tunic and we'll each hold a corner, and then Roo and Tigger can jump into it. They won't hurt themselves."

When Roo understood what he had to do, he was wildly excited, and cried out: "Tigger, we're going to jump! Tigger! Like flying, my jumping will be. Can Tiggers do it?" And he squeaked out: "I'm coming, Christopher Robin!" and he jumped – straight into the middle of the tunic.

He bounced and bounced – and went on bouncing and saying "Oo!" for quite a long time.

"Come on, Tigger," he called out. "It's easy."

But Tigger was holding on to the branch.

"Just wait a moment," said Tigger nervously. "Small piece of bark in my eye." And he moved slowly along his branch.

And suddenly Tigger found how easy it was.

"Ow!" he shouted as the tree flew past him.

"Look out!" cried Christopher Robin to the others.

There was a crash, and a tearing noise, and a confused heap of everybody on the ground.

Underneath everybody else was Eeyore.

"Oh, Eeyore!" cried Christopher Robin. "Are you hurt?"

Eeyore said nothing for a long time. And then he said: "Is Tigger there?"

Tigger was there, feeling Bouncy again already.

"Yes," said Christopher Robin. "Tigger's here."

"Well, just thank him for me," said Eeyore.

Tigger is Unbounced

One day Rabbit and Piglet were sitting outside Pooh's front
door listening to Rabbit, and Pooh was sitting with them. It
was a drowsy summer afternoon, so Pooh got into a comfortable
position for not listening to Rabbit, and from time to time he
opened his eyes to say "Ah!" and then closed them again to say
"True," and from time to time Rabbit said, "You see what I
mean, Piglet," very earnestly, and Piglet nodded earnestly to
show that he did.

"In fact," said Rabbit, coming to the end of it at last, "Tigger's getting so Bouncy nowadays that it's time we taught him a lesson. Don't you think so, Piglet?"

Piglet said that Tigger was very Bouncy, and that if they could think of a way of unbouncing him it would be a Very Good Idea.

"Well, I've got an idea," said Rabbit, "and here it is. We take Tigger for a long explore, somewhere where he's never been, and we lose him there, and next morning we find him again, and – mark my words – he'll be a different Tigger altogether."

"Why?" said Pooh.

"Because he'll be a Humble Tigger. Because he'll be a Sad Tigger, a Melancholy Tigger, a Small and Sorry Tigger, an Oh-Rabbit-I-*am*-glad-to-see-you Tigger. That's why."

"I should hate him to go *on* being Sad," said Piglet doubtfully.

"Tiggers never go on being Sad," explained Rabbit. "They get over it with Astonishing Rapidity. But if we can make Tigger feel Small and Sad just for five minutes, we shall have done a good deed."

So it was arranged that they should start next morning.

The next day was quite a different day. Instead of being hot and sunny, it was cold and misty. But when Piglet and Pooh got to Rabbit's house, Rabbit said it was just the day for them, because Tigger always bounced on ahead of everybody, and as soon as he got out of sight, they would hurry away in the other direction, and he would never see them again.

"Not never?" said Piglet.

"Well, not until we find him again, Piglet. Tomorrow, or whenever it is. Come on. He's waiting for us."

When they got to Kanga's house, they found that Roo was waiting too, being a great friend of Tigger's, which made it Awkward; but Rabbit whispered "Leave this to me" behind his paw to Pooh, and went up to Kanga.

"I don't think Roo had better come," he said. "Not today."

"Why not?" said Roo, who wasn't supposed to be listening.

"Nasty cold day," said Rabbit, shaking his head. "And you were coughing this morning."

"Oh, Roo, you never told me," said Kanga reproachfully.

"It was a biscuit cough," said Roo, "not one you tell about."

"I think not today, dear. Another day."

So off they went, without Roo.

At first Pooh and Rabbit and Piglet walked together, and Tigger ran round them in circles, and then, when the path got narrower, Rabbit, Piglet and Pooh walked one after another, and Tigger ran up and down in front of them, and sometimes he bounced into Rabbit and sometimes he didn't.

And as they got higher, the mist got thicker, so that Tigger kept disappearing, and then when you thought he wasn't there, there he was again, saying, "I say, come on," and before you could say anything, there he wasn't.

Rabbit turned round and nudged Piglet.

"The next time," he said. "Tell Pooh."

"The next time," said Piglet to Pooh.

"The next what?" said Pooh to Piglet.

Tigger appeared suddenly, bounced into Rabbit, and disappeared again. "Now!" said Rabbit. He jumped into a hollow by the side of the path, and Pooh and Piglet jumped after him. They crouched in the bracken, listening.

The Forest was very silent when you stopped and listened to it. They could see nothing and hear nothing.

"H'sh!" said Rabbit.

"I am," said Pooh.

There was a pattering noise ... then silence again.

"Hallo!" said Tigger, and he sounded so close suddenly that Piglet would have jumped if Pooh hadn't accidentally been sitting on most of him.

"Where are you?" called Tigger.

"That's funny," said Tigger.

There was a moment's silence, and then they heard him pattering off again.

"Well?" Rabbit whispered proudly. "There we are! Just as I said."

And they all hurried off, Rabbit leading the way.

"Why are we going along here?" said Pooh, after a little while had passed.

"Because it's the way home," Rabbit said confidently.

"Oh!" said Pooh.

"I *think* it's more to the right," said Piglet nervously. "What do *you* think, Pooh?"

Pooh looked at his two paws. He knew that one of them was the right, and he knew that when you had decided which one of them was the right, then the other one was the left, but he never could remember how to begin.

"Well —" he said slowly.

"Come on," said Rabbit. "I know it's this way."

They went on. Ten minutes later they stopped again.

"It's a funny thing," said Rabbit, "how everything looks the same in a mist. Have you noticed it, Pooh?"

Pooh said that he had.

"Lucky we know the Forest so well, or we might get lost,"
said Rabbit half an hour later, and he gave the careless
laugh which you give when you know the Forest so well
that you can't get lost.

Piglet sidled up to Pooh from behind.

"Pooh!" he whispered.

"Yes, Piglet?"

"Nothing," said Piglet, taking Pooh's paw. "I just wanted
to be sure of you."

When Tigger had finished waiting for the others to catch him up, he thought he would go home. So he trotted back; and the first thing Kanga said when she saw him was, "There's a good Tigger. You're just in time for your Strengthening Medicine," and she poured it out for him.

"Now then, run along," said Kanga.
"Where shall we run along to?" asked Roo.
"You can go and collect some fir-cones for me," said Kanga, giving them a basket.

So they went to the Six Pine Trees, and threw fir-cones at
each other until they had forgotten what they came for, and
they left the basket under the trees and went back to dinner.
And it was just as they were finishing dinner that
Christopher Robin put his head in at the door.

"Where's Pooh?" he asked.
"Tigger dear, where's Pooh?" said Kanga.

Tigger explained what had happened at the same time that Roo was explaining about his Biscuit Cough and Kanga was telling them not both to talk at once, so it was some time before Christopher Robin guessed that Pooh and Piglet and Rabbit were all lost in the mist on the top of the Forest.

"Well," said Christopher Robin, "we shall have to go and find them, that's all. Come on, Tigger."

* * * *

"The fact is," said Rabbit, "we've missed our way somehow."

They were having a rest in a small sand-pit on the top of the Forest. Pooh was getting rather tired of that sand-pit, and suspected it of 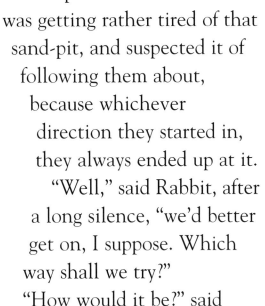 following them about, because whichever direction they started in, they always ended up at it.

"Well," said Rabbit, after a long silence, "we'd better get on, I suppose. Which way shall we try?"

"How would it be?" said Pooh slowly, "if, as soon as we're out of sight of this Pit, we try to find it again?"

"What's the good of that?" said Rabbit. "If I walked away from this Pit, and then walked back to it, of *course* I should find it."

"Well, I thought perhaps you wouldn't," said Pooh. "I just thought."

"Try," said Piglet suddenly. "We'll wait here for you."

Rabbit gave a laugh to show how silly Piglet was, and walked into the mist. After he had gone a hundred yards, he turned and walked back again . . . and after Pooh and Piglet had waited twenty minutes for him, Pooh got up.

"I just thought," said Pooh. "Now then, Piglet, let's go home."

"But, Pooh," cried Piglet, all excited, "do you know the way?"

"No," said Pooh. "But there are twelve pots of honey in my cupboard, and they've been calling to me for hours. I couldn't hear them properly before because Rabbit *would* talk, but if nobody says anything except those twelve pots, I *think*, Piglet, I shall know where they're coming from. Come on."

They walked off together; and for a long time Piglet said nothing, so as not to interrupt the pots; and then suddenly he made a squeaky noise... and an oo-noise... because now he began to know where he was; but he still didn't dare to say so out loud, in case he wasn't. And just when he was getting so sure of himself that it didn't matter whether the pots went on calling or not, there was a shout from in front of them, and out of the mist came Christopher Robin.

"Oh, there you are," said Christopher Robin carelessly, trying to pretend that he hadn't been Anxious.

"Here we are," said Pooh.

"Where's Rabbit?"

"I don't know," said Pooh.

"Oh – well, I expect Tigger will find him. He's sort of looking for you all."

"Well," said Pooh, "I've got to go home for something, and so has Piglet, because we haven't had it yet, and —"

"I'll come and watch you," said Christopher Robin.

So he went home with Pooh, and watched him for quite a
long time... and all the time he was watching, Tigger was
tearing round the Forest making loud yapping noises for Rabbit.
And at last a very Small and Sorry Rabbit heard him.

And the Small and Sorry Rabbit rushed through the mist at the noise, and it suddenly turned into Tigger; a Friendly Tigger, a Grand Tigger, a Large and Helpful Tigger, a Tigger who bounced, if he bounced at all, in just the beautiful way a Tigger ought to bounce.

"Oh, Tigger, I *am* glad to see you," cried Rabbit.